Jared and the Ordinary, Handy-dandy, Excellent, Extraordinary, Plain Brown String

A story about the joy of sharing

Written by Dana Webb

Illustrated by Mark McCord

Chariot Victor Publishing
A Division of Cook Communications

Chariot Victor Publishing
a division of Cook Communications, Colorado Springs, Colorado 80918
Cook Communications, Paris, Ontario
Kingsway Communications, Eastbourne, England

JARED AND THE ORDINARY, HANDY-DANDY, EXCELLENT, EXTRAORDINARY, PLAIN BROWN STRING
© 1999 by Dana Webb for text and Mark McCord for illustrations

Cover designed by Andrea Boven and Kelly Robinson
Edited by Kathy Davis
First hardcover printing, 1999
Printed in Singapore
03 02 01 00 99   5 4 3 2 1

Library of Congress Cataloging-in-Publication Data
Webb, Dana.
      Jared and the Ordinary, Handy-dandy, Excellent, Extraordinary, Plain Brown String/
written by Dana Webb; illustrated by Mark McCord.
                  p.   cm.
      Summary: A mother challenges her children to make something more
valuable out of three simple objects--a box, brown paper, and a piece of string.
      ISBN 0-7814-3052-6
      [1. Sharing--Fiction.   2. Christian life--Fiction.]   I. McCord,
Mark, ill. II. Title.
PZ7.W365Br1999
[E]--dc21
                                                          98-41776
                                                            CIP
                                                            AC

Dedication

This book is dedicated to our grandmother, Momo (Lucille Wiseman Enright), who could make do with little, make little go far, and bring smiles to all who received her clever creations.

Illustrator's Note

The artwork in this book is not computer generated. Backgrounds were painted with traditional brushes and paints. Foreground characters were hand-squeezed from a squeeze bottle filled with liquid rubber. The rubber colors were applied wet on wet and allowed to dry. The cured rubber was then peeled up and applied to the backgrounds. Dramatic lighting was used to photograph each illustration to enhance the 3-D nature of the rubber characters.

"Look," Mike announced, "the mailman's bringing us a package. Maybe it's a present or something cool."

Mom stood behind the three children and murmured, "Hmmm, I wonder if it's my birthday present?"

The package *was* for mom. "Hurry, Mom! Open it," Jared blurted out.

Mom untied the string, carefully removed the paper
without tearing it, and finally opened the box.
It was only a dress.
Mike groaned. Carly rolled her eyes.
Jared sighed.

Mom looked at their disappointed faces and announced, "Hey, I have an idea. Even though it's my birthday, I'm going to give you some gifts. Carly, you take the paper. Mike, here's the box. And you, Jared, can have the brown string. Let's see if you can take something simple and make it more valuable. At the end of the day, we'll have show and tell, and you can show everyone how you made your gift even better!"

Carly smiled as she marched to her room and shut the door.

Mike burst out, "I know what I'm doing!" as he ran down the hall to his room.

Jared wasn't sure what to do with a piece of ordinary brown string. He went to his room and found an old toy boat and the only scissors he was allowed to use. They were squeaky, had rounded tips, and didn't cut very well.

Jared went outside. He would tie the string to his boat and pull it on the pond. Would that make his string more valuable?

Jared's neighbor, Mr. Leon, was working in his garden. "Hey, Jared, tell me something new." Mr. Leon always said that.

Jared sighed. "I'm supposed to think of ways to make this string better than it is now."

"Well, if I had that string right now, I know what I'd do," Mr. Leon replied. "I need to make a new flower bed. To draw a straight line on the grass I would push small sticks into the ground and tie string at the top of the sticks. Then I would use the string as a guide for my shovel."

"Here, you can use my string," Jared said as he handed it to Mr. Leon.

Jared helped tie the string to the sticks, then he watched Mr. Leon place the shovel exactly under the string and push down, cutting through the grass. Then Mr. Leon began digging a flower bed with straight, even sides.

"Thanks, Jared!" said Mr. Leon. "That's a handy-dandy string you have there."

Jared felt good about sharing his string. He still had plenty left to pull his boat.

As he walked on down the sidewalk, he heard someone crying. Sitting near the sidewalk was a little girl. "What's wrong?" Jared asked.

"A big dog chased my cat up the tree, then he took her favorite toy and ran away," she sobbed.

"Maybe your cat would like to play with some string!" Jared said excitedly.

The girl stopped crying as she watched Jared cut a piece of string the perfect size for a cat.

Jared felt like a magician as he said, "Watch this!"

He held the string up and dangled it in front of the cat. She pawed playfully at it as Jared lured her down the tree trunk to the ground. Then she crouched low, leaped, and rolled. The string wiggled and danced over her head. The cat flipped and flopped trying to catch the string in her paws.

When the little girl started laughing, Jared handed her the string. "Here, it's your turn," he said.

"This is the best cat toy ever," she said.

Jared started to the pond again, but soon noticed Matthew Brown bending down on the sidewalk. Matthew was on the high school track team and often jogged past Jared's house.

He looked up and said, "Hi, Jared. I just broke my shoestring. I'm trying to use this broken piece, but it's a little too short."

"I have some string right here. Just cut off what you need," said Jared. He was happy that he could help another person with his string.

"Hey, that just might work!" Matthew began to cut the string and laughed. "These safety scissors sure are full of safety!" He threaded the string through the holes in his sneaker and made a secure knot. Then he jumped up and down to see if the string would hold.

"Thanks a lot, Jared!" he called as he waved good-bye and jogged down the sidewalk.

At the pond Jared tied the string to his boat and pulled it across the shallow water. It was fun, but not as much fun as he had thought it would be.

His string had been more fun when Mr. Leon had needed it to dig a flower bed, and when the little girl's cat had needed a new toy, and when Matthew had needed a shoestring. You sure could do a lot with a little bit of string!

Jared began walking home, dragging the string behind him. All that was left now was a piece that was about as long as Jared was tall. He was wondering what else he could do with it when he heard a voice.

"I saw you playing with your boat on the pond. I did the same thing when I was your age."

Jared looked up at the house across the street. Suddenly a lady with a vine draped over her shoulders appeared from behind a white post. It was Mrs. Olson from church. She laughed. "Hello, Jared! I'm trying to get this vine to grow around this post, but it keeps falling down."

Jared held up his string. "You could use this string to tie that vine to the post."

"Well, aren't you the smart one. I'm glad you showed up!" Mrs. Olson was as nice as Jared's grandmother.

Jared circled the post with the string and cut it off to the right length. Only a small piece was left. "It's almost all used up," Jared said as he laid his scissors and the last piece of string on the grass.

Jared helped Mrs. Olson tie the vine to the post. "I think that's going to do it!" she said. "I sure appreciate—" Before she could finish the sentence, she and Jared both gasped.

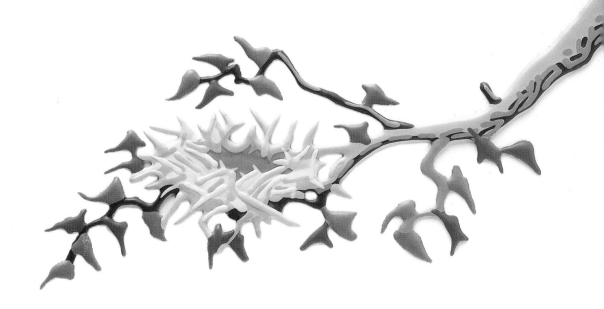

A bird swooped down, grabbed the last piece of string, and flew to the nearest tree.

Mrs. Olson nodded. "Well, I guess little Mama bird was looking for just the right string to add to her nest. She's been busy for days grabbing twigs and sticks. That string was probably like a special present to her."

"Like a birthday present?" Jared asked.

"Sure. Your string came in pretty handy around here today, young man. We both thank you!"

Jared smiled as he headed to his house. He had no string left—not even one little piece—but he'd had one of the best days ever!"

Mom greeted Jared at the door. "Hi, honey! Did you have fun at the pond? It's time for show and tell, remember?" Jared had forgotten about the show and tell part.

Carly came bustling into the room. "See how I used the paper to make a birthday card and wrapping paper. I decorated it with balloon stickers, and I drew the candles and party hats."

Jared was impressed. She had made something valuable from plain old paper.

"That's a great use for the paper," mom said as dad nodded in approval.

"Look at this!" Mike shouted as he pulled three small boxes from behind his back. He had colored hammers and saws all over the boxes. "Dad can put nails in this one, and screws in this one, and bolts in this one," bragged Mike.

"You did a very good job with the box," mom said as she patted Mike on the back. Dad agreed, "These boxes will sure help me out, Son." Jared thought the boxes looked very valuable.

Everyone looked at Jared as he stood there with no string. "Show us what you did with your string," Carly teased.

"Yeah, Jared, where's your string?" asked Mike. Carly and Mike stopped teasing Jared when mom spoke up. "This is show and tell. Maybe Jared is going to *tell* us about his string."

Jared nodded as if that had been his plan all along. "I was going to use my string to pull my boat on the pond, but Mr. Leon needed some right then! So we tied the string on sticks to make a straight line for his shovel. He made a new flower bed. He said the string was handy-dandy."

"That's lovely, Jared," said mom. "I think you—"

"But there's more," Jared continued.

"A little girl was crying 'cause a big dog stole her cat's toy. We used the string to make a new toy for the cat!"

"That's an excellent use for the string, Jared," mom said.

"But I'm not through," Jared insisted. "Matthew had a broken shoestring. I gave him some string so he could tie his shoe and start running again."

"Extraordinary," said dad.

"But that's not all," Jared said. "I did pull my boat in the water, but not for long. I helped Mrs. Olson tie her vine around the post on her porch."

"Hmmm. All that from a plain brown string," mom murmured.

"Just one more thing," Jared continued. "A mama bird took my last piece of string for her nest. Mrs. Olson said that the string was like a present for the bird. Does that make it valuable, Mom?"

Mom said, "Yes, Jared. You used your string to help others. You made it even more valuable than when it was tied around my present!"

Dad agreed, "I think you sure got the goodness out of that string!"

Jared was very proud.

Dad looked at the three children. "You kids all did an excellent job of making some simple things even more valuable than they were before. Carly, your paper will brighten someone's birthday. Mike, your boxes will help me keep my workshop neat. And Jared, you gave all of your string to help others. Well done. Now, who wants birthday cake?"

Faith Parenting Guide

Jared and the Ordinary, Handy-dandy, Excellent, Extraordinary, Plain Brown String
A Story about the Joy of Sharing

Ages: 4-7

Life Issue: My child doesn't always want to share with or help others.

Spiritual Building Blocks: Sharing/Resourcefulness

And do not forget to do good and to share with others, for with such sacrifices God is pleased (Heb. 13:16).

Visual Learning Style: After reading the story, ask your child to go through the book and count all the people (and animals) that Jared helped. Give your child a piece of string and ask her to find at least one new way to use it to help someone around your house. Have show and tell.

Auditory Learning Style: Ask your child to think of a time when he helped someone. Now ask him to think of a time when he didn't help. Ask how he felt each time. Say, "Jared found lots of good uses for a simple string. God has given us many things. Can you think of some things God has given you that you can use to help others?" (Help your child think of not only money and things, but talents as well.) Ask: "How can sharing (the item) make it more valuable?" Discuss practical ways to share your resources or talents as a family. For example: help an elderly neighbor pull weeds; baby-sit so a mom can run an errand; feed a friend's cat while she's out of town; pass down some good used clothes or toys to a child who needs them, and so on.

Tactile Learning Style: Empty a bag of candy or other treats (coins, small toys, and so on) in the center of your family circle and tell your kids they can take as much as they like. Don't interfere as they divide the loot. (If you are doing this activity with only one child, see if she keeps all the goodies or shares with you.) When the goodies are divided, whether fairly or not, discuss:
- When I said you could take as much as you wanted, what did you do?
- Do you think you were selfish or unselfish?
- How do you think the rest of the family feels about the way the goodies were divided?
- How do your actions prove whether or not you're selfish?
- How is showing your love by serving others the opposite of being selfish?

The tactile learning activity is adapted from *Family Night Tool Chest: An Introduction to Family Nights* by Jim Weidmann and Kurt Bruner, 1997, Chariot Victor Publishing, pp. 47-48.